Hug in the Wind

by Tim Steiner

First Printing, 2018
Drawn Digitally
ISBN 978-1-7321902-0-7

Find Tim Steiner on Facebook and Instagram @RoundelBooks
www.roundelbooks.com

For Andrew:
Your goodbye hug inspired it all.

And for every military child
awaiting a sweet reunion.

Nothing was harder than saying goodbye.

Watching you wave as I left to fly.

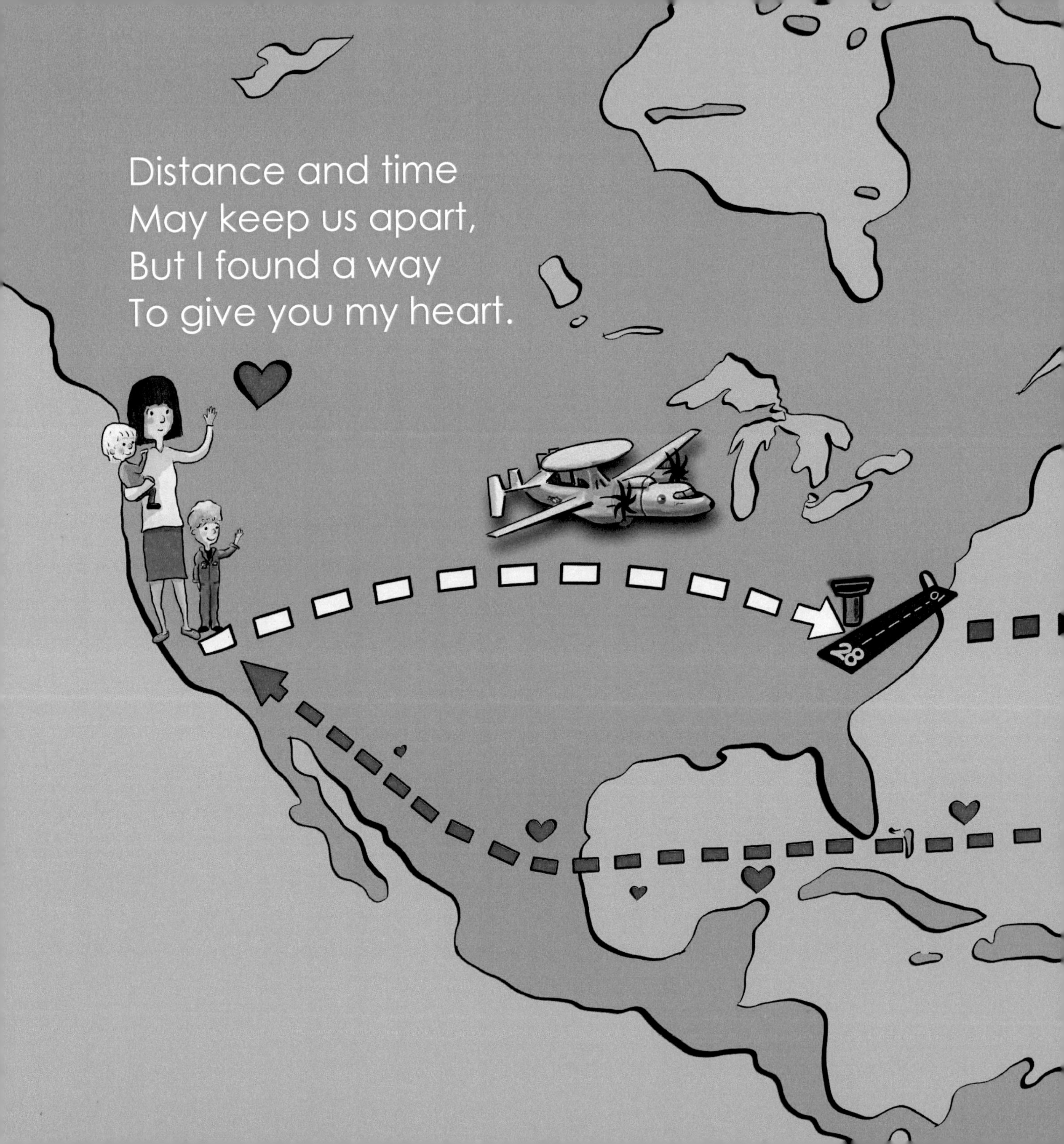

Distance and time
May keep us apart,
But I found a way
To give you my heart.

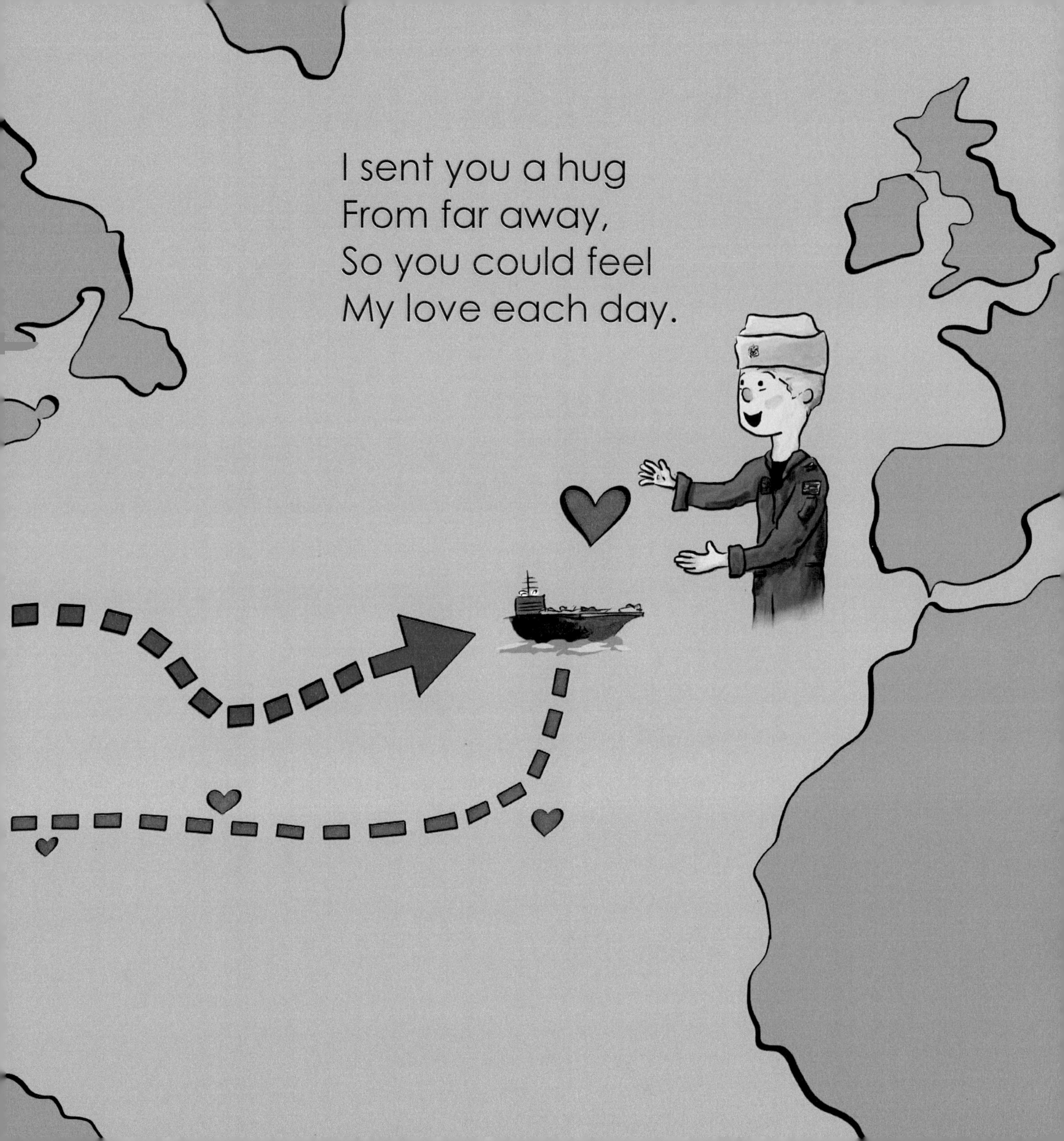

I sent you a hug
From far away,
So you could feel
My love each day.

I stood at the front of my very big ship,
The place I have been for my very long trip.

I stretched out my arms big and wide,
And thought of my love for you deep inside.

You might ask,

"How do you package a hug
That you send?"

You see, my child...

I wrapped my hug in the wind!

600

The wind carried my hug
From the ship 'cross the sea.

Then over dry land
Where lions run free.

My hug helped blow a bright kite in the air,

Then it went with the wind
Through a lady's long hair!

Up mountains steep,

And down valleys deep,
The wind zipped along with a delivery to keep!

Although there are many things
The wind had to do,

It still found a way to bring my hug to you!

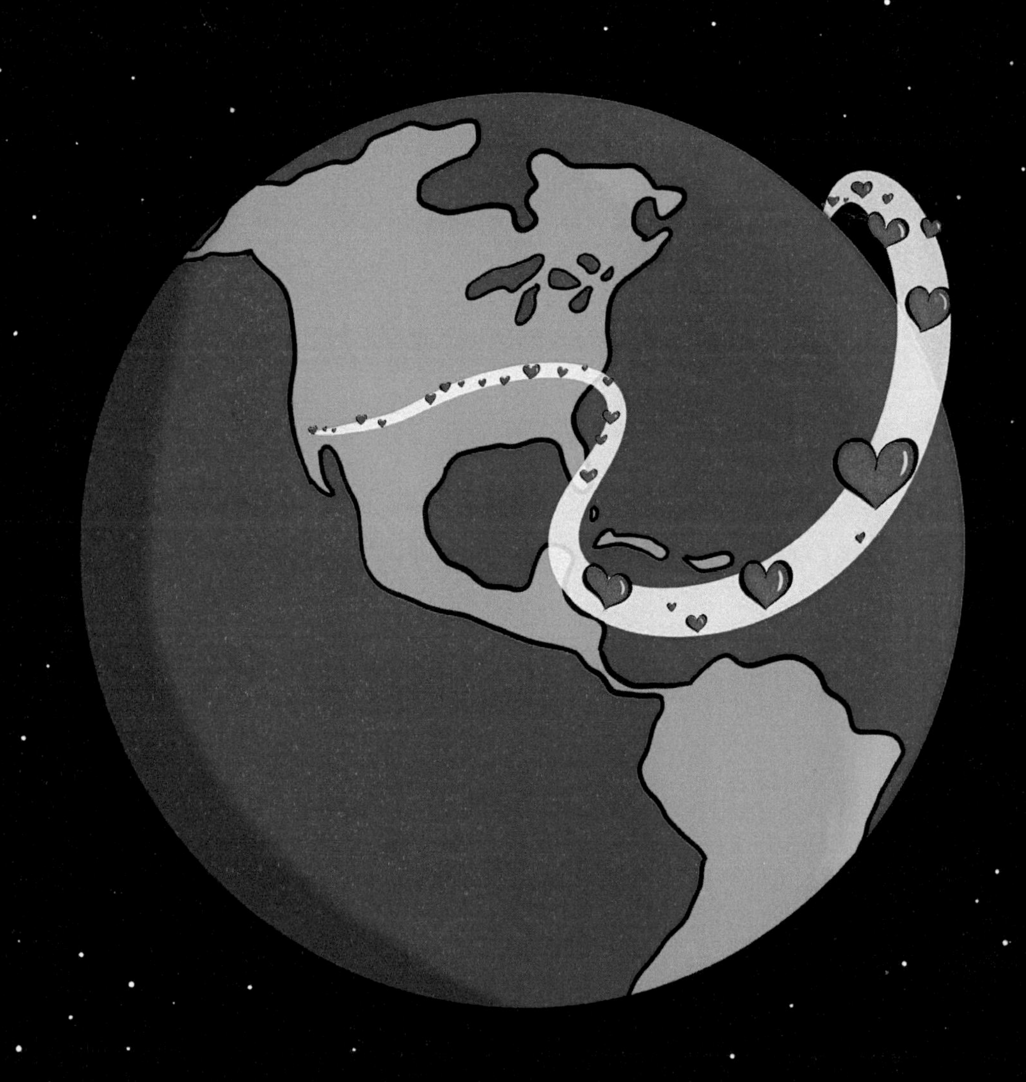

You feel it on your skin
When you run quickly outside.

Or you hear it hit the house
When you watch from inside.

It lifts birds and planes,
As they fly through the air,

And now it can help
You know that I care.

The wind brought my hug,
From me, **just for you.**

When you feel the wind,
It is **our hug...**

I feel it, too.

The End

Thank you so much for reading *Hug in the Wind*. If you are currently separated from a loved-one, I hope this book touches your heart.

While deployed two years ago, I wrote and illustrated this story for Andrew's second birthday—the second birthday I would miss in two years. The project took two months. I woke up early every morning before my flights to draw each page. It was therapy. Writing and drawing connected me to Alison and Andrew, knowing they would spend time with each page I made.

You may notice that the story shows a family with two kids. When I made the original *Hug in the Wind*, my daughter hadn't yet arrived. We found out Alison was pregnant with Claire two nights before I deployed—surprise! Thankfully, I made it home one week before Claire was born. I include her in this updated version.

Hug in the Wind holds a special place with my family—I truly hope it blesses your family, too. Sincerely, Tim Steiner

Also by Tim Steiner:

If you like my stories, please tell others!
Write reviews on amazon.com!

About the Author and Illustrator:

Tim Steiner grew up in Corvallis, Oregon and graduated from the United States Naval Academy in 2010. *Hug in the Wind* was his first children's book and catalyst for his publishing company, Roundel Books. He lives in Virginia with his loving wife, their two curious kids, and their Golden Retriever, Stella.

Follow him on Facebook and Instagram **@roundelbooks** and visit **RoundelBooks.com**

Made in the USA
San Bernardino, CA
03 July 2018